Best wishes
Daniel Morden

SECRET TALES
from WALES

DANIEL MORDEN
illustrated by BRETT BRECKON

Gomer

For Marion – D. M.

First published in 2017 by Gomer Press,
Llandysul, Ceredigion SA44 4JL

Hardback ISBN 978 1 78562 221 2

Paperback version first published 2019
ISBN 978 1 78562 321 9

A CIP record for this title is available from the British Library.

The author wishes to acknowledge the award of a
Literature Wales Writer's Bursary supported by the
National Lottery through Arts Council of Wales
for the purposes of completing this book.

This book is published with the financial support of the
Welsh Books Council.

Printed and bound in Wales at
Gomer Press, Llandysul, Ceredigion
www.gomer.co.uk

༄

Enough for one,
Too much for two,
Nothing for three.
What is it?

༄

Contents

Secret Tales

There lived in Abergavenny a great magician. It was said he knew every tongue spoken by man or woman on this wide earth. He knew the languages of the birds and the beasts and the insects. He knew where the wind came from and where it was going. He knew why the sky was high and why the earth lay below. He knew how many angels there were in heaven. He knew their names and the roles that the Creator had given them. He knew all the mysteries of Hell as well. He knew how to summon an evil thing, how to bend that devil to his will, and how to send the infernal creature back into the fiery depths where it belonged.

All of these secrets were kept in an enormous leather book. Fixed to the front of the book was an iron padlock. The magician kept the key on a chain around his neck. Whenever he was apart from it he kept the book locked, for fear that someone might read these precious secrets.

The magician hired a local lad, a farmer's son, to do his errands.

On his first day in the magician's employment, the magician led the lad into the study. The boy was dumbstruck. What a jumble of wonders! Crucibles, candles and cauldrons, books, bowls and bones, shelves of skulls, clawed creatures curled in jars, heady roots hanging from the roof beams, bottles of lotions and potions.

The magician stood the lad before the leather-bound book and said, 'If ever you find this open, do not read it. This book is full of secrets. They are not for you. They are for me and me only. Do you understand?'

A lifetime of learning and yet still the magician knew nothing of human nature! The lad had had no interest in the book until that moment. He had been overwhelmed by the exotic paraphernalia that surrounded it. But now the rest of the room vanished.

His head was filled with whispers:

'What secrets hide within the book?
What mysteries are answered?
What harm would there be in taking a look?
Just a little look …'

Some said the magician could summon the dead from their dank, dark beds. Some said he could see far-off lands through a black mirror. Some said he could turn rock into gold. The magician travelled, yet he had no horse. Perhaps hiding between those covers was a spell to grant the power of flight.

The days turned to weeks. The weeks turned to months. The magician was always busy, peering at his book, muttering to himself, rushing this way and that. Sometimes he would grow angry with the lad for some little thing. Sometimes the magician would be pleased, and reward him by telling a wonderful tale.

The whispering in the lad's head grew louder. If ever the magician was out, the lad's eyes would stray toward the study.

Then the magician was called away suddenly. The lad was alone in the house. The whispers overwhelmed him:

'He keeps all of that knowledge to himself.

Where's the justice in that?

What does he do with this power?

A compendium of marvels, but have you ever seen him cast a single spell?

Just a glimpse at the pages …

What could possibly go wrong?'

The lad crept into the study.

In his haste the magician had left the book open.

The lad glimpsed movement. He sidled closer. To his astonishment he saw the words wriggling, squirming and twisting on the page.

Another whisper:

'Free me!'

He cast about.

'Here! Down here! Free me!'

On the page before him he read the words:

'Here! Down here! Free me!'

'How?'

The letters formed into another sentence:

'Just read me!'

In his ear:

'Just read me!'

Before he knew what he was doing, the lad had read the words aloud.

The light in the room thickened. The house trembled. A clap of thunder. The shadows formed into a figure with eyes like blazing coals. The air was acrid smoke. The lad's eyes streamed. He choked.

That voice again …

'What do you please?'

'What?'

'For three centuries I have been a captive between the pages of the book, but you have freed me. I was a character in a tale, a puppet for the

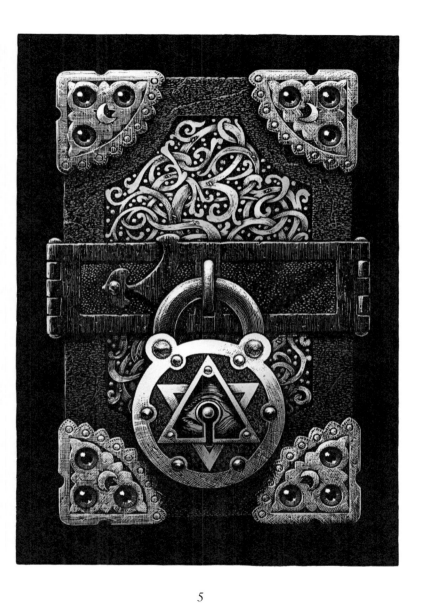

author to play with … I had to live out the same stupid story every day for three hundred years, but now that I am real, I am no longer chained by words! In return for freeing me, I must do your bidding. When you can think of no more tasks for me, I am free to make my own story. Begin!'

The lad's mind went blank. He opened his mouth and nothing came out. The thing grinned. It rose over him. The lad shuddered.

'Give me a task, or I am free!'

'Sweep the yard!'

The creature was gone – then it was back, and bigger.

'Done. Another task!'

'Build a wall around it!'

The creature was gone – then it was back, and bigger still.

'Another!'

'Mend the leaks in the roof.'

Whoosh! Back in a flash. Even bigger and even closer.

'Another.'

The lad stammered.

'Dig a well.'

That should keep him busy …

Whoosh! The thing was so close now the lad could feel its foul breath.

'*Another.*'

'Count the blades of grass in my master's field.'

'*Four million, three hundred thousand, nine hundred and twenty seven.*'

It stretched out its scaly claw toward him …

The door burst open. The magician cried, 'Thing of shadows! This lad is my servant, so you must do my bidding!'

'*Until you can think of no more tasks. What is your pleasure?*'

'Count all the words in the Bible in Saint Mary's Church!'

The beast roared. '*But I cannot enter a holy place!*'

'If you cannot complete the task I have given you, then you must return to the book.'

'*Damn you!*' and it vanished. The magician slammed the book shut and locked it.

'I told you not to read the book! If that thing had been free, terrible things would have happened!'

'So the book is a prison?'

'It is full of stories. Stories are spells. They are alive. They can change the world. They long to be spoken, so they can roam again. Some make us hope, some make us hate. Be careful what you speak. Words can bless or burn.'

Black Robin

Is it better to be born lucky or clever? There once lived a poor man. Because he was a charcoal burner, he was known as Robin Ddu, or Black Robin. He was as thin as a stick. He was so broke he boiled his shoes for soup. Every Friday evening, after market was over, he went to town and searched the street for whatever vegetables had been left behind. Once he was crawling in the gutter when a gold coin dropped before him. Robin looked up and saw a pair of shiny boots. On top of the boots were a pair of tailored trousers. On top of the tailored trousers a bronze-buckled belt. On top of the belt a silken shirt. A gentleman in a velvet cloak loomed over him.

'Thank you!' said Robin. 'Tell me, what kind of business has brought you such wealth?'

'Business? My friend, you are mistaken. I'm far too honest to be a businessman. I am a thief.'

'So what kind of thievery pays so well?'

'You remind me of me. I was once down on my luck, so I will tell you a secret. I bought myself a cloak, a crystal ball and a couple of old books and proclaimed myself to be the finest magician in the world. Now, folk beg me to solve their problems. When they are desperate, people will believe anything. Why not do the same?'

'Why not indeed? Thank you, brother!'

'Here, have my cloak. I'll buy another!'

Robin walked to a town where no one knew him, and painted a sign which read: 'The Wise Wizard of the West'. He sat in the market place, muttering under his breath and making strange signs in the air. Very quickly, word spread through the town about a remarkable stranger with miraculous powers. The mayor sent for him.

'Welcome, oh wise wizard! I have a private matter I hope you can help me with.'

Robin hadn't eaten more than a stale crust of bread for a fortnight.

'I can't enchant on an empty stomach …'

'Then tonight you dine with me!'

A trickle of drool dribbled out of the corner of Robin's mouth. 'What are we having?'

'Oh, I don't know,' said the mayor, 'I leave it to the servants. And I am afraid there will be only three courses.'

'Three courses?' He was so excited he couldn't keep up his pretence of wisdom. All the way to the mayor's mansion, all Robin could say was, 'Three courses!'

So the mayor grew suspicious. 'This is just some rogue after a free meal! I'll put him to the test.'

He summoned one of his servants. The mayor whispered in the servant's ear, then said to Robin, 'Great mage, I can't wait any longer to see you in action! Before we eat, I wonder if you would be kind enough to give me a demonstration of your remarkable powers.'

The wise wizard went white. 'I am not some conjurer who pulls rabbits out of hats, you know.'

'Of course, but surely a task as simple as this,' he clapped, and a plate covered with a large bowl was brought in, 'will be easy for one so skilled in the mystic arts. Tell me, what is under the bowl?'

The wise wizard put his face in his hands. He shook his head and said, 'Robin, they've caught you!'

The mayor gasped! The servants cried out in wonder! The bowl was lifted to reveal a robin pecking at the plate.

'Astonishing!' said the mayor. 'Please forgive me for doubting your magical abilities! Listen to me now. Someone has stolen a precious jewel. I'll pay you in gold to locate the thief.'

Robin's belly gurgled. 'What about the three courses?'

'Ah! Forgive me!'

The mayor clapped his hands again. In came a waiter with a tray and two bowls of steaming soup. If Robin had been more observant, perhaps he would have spotted the waiter was trembling. You see, he and the other three waiters were the thieves.

At last he could eat! Robin couldn't control his excitement. He cried out, 'There's the first!'

CRASH! The waiter dropped the tray and bolted back into the kitchen. 'He knows!'

'Don't be ridiculous! How could he possibly know?' said the second waiter. 'Get out there with more soup before they suspect something!'

So the first servant took out two more bowls, shaking from head to foot. Robin, ravenous, watched the servant's every step.

Once he was back in the kitchen the first servant said to the second, 'I can't go back to the table. He stared at me so intently I could feel him peering into my soul!'

'Pah! Nonsense! Leave this to me.'

The soup wasn't enough for Robin, so when the next course appeared – plates of roast beef, mashed potato, carrots, peas and horseradish sauce – he stood up and cried, 'Ah! There's the second!'

The waiter stumbled.

'What's wrong with you people today?' said the mayor.

'I beg your pardon your honour. I … slipped on some soup.'

He staggered back into the kitchen and hissed to his fellows, 'You were right! But how could this wizard possibly know our secret?'

'You pair of spineless cowards!' said the third. 'He doesn't know a thing! Watch this!'

Robin liked the starter, he enjoyed the main course, but the dessert was his favourite. 'Any minute now!' he thought, licking his lips. 'I hope there's custard!'

So when a waiter emerged from the kitchen with a choice of steaming puddings, Robin leapt to his feet, clapped his hands, and cried, 'Here comes the third!'

The waiter went as white as a candle. It was all he could do to stay upright. As soon as he was back in the kitchen he said to the others, 'You were right! He knows everything!'

'If he is so wise, how come he hasn't mentioned me?' said the fourth.

After a big meal Robin liked to smoke, so he went to the fireplace beside the kitchen for a flame. He rummaged in his bag for his pipe. He searched and searched until, exasperated, he cried, 'I know you're in there – come out at once!'

Behind the kitchen door, the fourth waiter's blood ran cold. He crept into the hall and beckoned Robin.

When they were alone with him, the waiters dropped to their knees and cried, 'All-seeing arch-mage, you have us at your mercy. If you tell the mayor the truth he will have us hanged for stealing the jewel! Think of our families!'

Robin was flabbergasted, but he assumed a stern expression and said, 'You should be ashamed of yourselves.'

They cowered even lower and whimpered even more.

'Bring me the jewel and a ball of dough.'

They did. He pushed the diamond into the dough and fed it to the mayor's goose.

Robin led the mayor out into the garden. 'There,' he said, pointing at the goose. 'There's your thief!'

They cut open the bird … and found the jewel!

'It must have fallen from your wife's dressing

table and been swept up by a servant. When the rubbish was thrown out, the goose found it and swallowed it!'

The mayor was overjoyed. He heaped gold upon the wise wizard and said, 'Truly, nothing is hidden from you!'

'Too true, too true. I have a gift from God.'

'It is as if you can see everything!'

'I can,' said Robin, thinking about dinner. 'I can see everything.'

'In that case, my wife is pregnant. Girl or a boy?'

'What?'

'I thought you could see everything!'

'I can, it is just that … she isn't here.'

'Servants! Fetch her!'

In came the mayor's wife. Robin's mind was racing.

'Walk up and down, would you please?'

She did. Robin said, 'When she comes towards me, I see a boy. When she walks away, a girl.'

Didn't the mayor's wife give birth to twins!

So, which was Robin – lucky or clever?

How Jack Found a Bride

On the border between England and Wales there lived a master mason. He was crafty. He could make anything, and make it beautiful. The things he made were as beautiful as he was ugly. His son, Jack, was the opposite of his father. The mason was ugly; Jack handsome. The mason clever; Jack, not so much.

One day, Jack said to his father, 'If you are so clever, can you make me some brains? How will I manage after you're gone?'

The mason had been pondering this problem himself. 'I can't make you brains. I am not God,' he said. 'But I can find you some. Take this fleece. Go to market. Sell it. Bring me back the skin and the worth of it.'

Jack scratched his head. How could he do that? But he was an obedient lad, so off he went.

As he crossed a bridge he saw a woman washing clothes in the river. Mary was her name. She looked up, saw him and stared. He was used to women staring at him. This one, Jack thought, was as lovely as the morning star.

'You up there,' she said. 'What is the matter?'

Jack told her about his father's instruction.

'Sell it to me.'

She sheared the wool from it and handed him back the skin.

Jack returned to his father.

'How did you do this?' he asked Jack.

'There was a woman under a bridge washing clothes. She saw me as I crossed. She told me what to do.'

'Would you know her again?'

Jack blushed and nodded.

'Tomorrow, I want you to find her and ask her this …'

Next day, Jack went to town, found Mary, and said, 'My father says: three people cross a bridge.

One of them sees it and touches it.

The second sees it but doesn't touch it.

The third neither sees it nor touches it.

How can this be?'

'It can be because …' and Mary told him the answer.

Jack returned to his father.

'She says the answer is …

It is a pregnant woman with a baby in her arms who crosses the bridge.

The woman sees and touches the bridge.

The baby sees it but doesn't touch it.

The child inside her neither sees nor touches it.'

'She's sharp, this one,' said Jack's father. What was her name?'

'Oh! I didn't think to ask it.'

'You didn't think to ask it!'

Next market day Jack and his father travelled into town as usual. As they walked the mason said, 'Shorten the road.'

'What?'

'Shorten the road.'

'How can I do that? The road is as short or as long as it is.'

The mason shook his head. He didn't say anything until they reached town.

'Be off with you, and don't come back until you can shorten the road home.'

Jack was at a loss what to do. As he walked through the market, didn't he see the woman from the bridge?

'Look at you!' she said. 'Why the long face?'

He told her his father's mysterious instruction.

'Ah!' she said. 'He wants you to tell him a story. If you are listening to a tale while you travel, the road seems shorter. Do you know any stories?'

'Only the ones he told me.'

'Why don't I tell you some your father won't know?'

'Thank you!'

When the market was over Jack found his father and said, 'I can shorten the road for you.'

'Go on then.'

The journey and the stories began.

There was once a king who was famous for his wisdom. He was loved by his people. He was young and strong and powerful, so his people were astonished when his heralds travelled the length and breadth of the land proclaiming:

'We are in grave danger. I cannot save this land. But there is one who could do so. This one must come to me not dressed and not naked, not riding and not walking, and must speak to me neither indoors nor outdoors. If this one does so, then the land can be saved. But if no one can, then we shall all be destroyed.'

Who could do these things?

Many tried and failed. In one corner of

19

the kingdom lived an old woman and her granddaughter. The grandmother had told the young woman stories every day of her life, so that now all the grandmother had to do was say, 'Like the robin under the bowl', and the child would know what story she was referring to. The granddaughter said to her grandmother, 'There must be a terrible threat for the king to speak in this way. I cannot stay here. I must try to help.'

And so it was that servants came to the king: 'Your majesty, a young woman says she can save the nation.'

'What are you waiting for? Bring her in.'

'Your majesty, she wants you to come to her.'

So the king made his way out of the throne room, and there, in the entrance, was a young woman, wrapped in a net, sitting on a goat with her feet dragging on either side.

'Well?'

'Well, what? Look!'

'At what?'

'Me. I am speaking to you neither inside nor outside.

I am not dressed, but not naked.

I am neither riding nor walking.'

'Ah! A wise woman told me only the one who could do these things could save the nation. You see,

21

a monster has set me three riddles. If I cannot solve them, he will kill me and take the throne.'

'Tell me the riddles, your highness.'

So the king did.

'Nothing is simpler!'

She gave him the answers.

He went to the monster. It was squatting on the branch of a tree. It saw the king and grinned. Its teeth were as sharp as needles. Its eyes were black as oil.

'I am glad to see you your majesty. I was getting hungry. Riddle me this! How many stars are there in the sky?'

'As many hairs as there are on your head. I'll count the stars while you pull out your hairs,' replied the king.

The monster growled. 'I will take your word for it. Answer me this, how high is the sky?'

'As high as you can kick yourself. If you don't believe me, prove me wrong!'

The monster bared his dripping fangs. 'Think carefully before you answer my third riddle. If I do not like your reply I will eat you alive. When will I die?'

'I have consulted the constellations and you will die half an hour after I do.'

The monster snarled. He stamped his clawed feet, but he didn't dare touch the king.

'One final test. I have dreamed my own death. I heard a voice as I slept. I cannot be killed by man nor beast. Not by day or night. I must be given a gift that is not a gift by someone who is neither eating nor not eating. No weapon can harm me. Send me the one who can kill me. Let them try. If they fail, I will eat you alive.'

The king told the young woman the final test.

'Leave this to me.' She went to the monster. She hid and watched him gorge himself on seven sheep, then climb up a tree and doze. When twilight came she cried, 'Wake up beast! I have come to kill you!'

The monster grunted and snorted and opened his red eyes 'How dare you wake me! I cannot be killed by man nor beast, but I can kill you! And I will!'

'I am neither man nor beast.'

The monster reddened.

'I cannot be killed by day or by night.'

'It is neither day nor night.'

The monster growled.

She held up something. 'Here, take this!'

Without thinking, he reached towards her. She opened her hand and out flew a dove.

'A gift that is not a gift!'

The monster lashed his long tail back and forth.

'But you must be neither eating nor not eating!'

'I am chewing a piece of tree bark!'

She grabbed his tail and tugged. The monster fell head first from the tree. His skull split and he was dead.

The young woman went back to the king. To thank her for saving the nation he arranged for her and her grandmother to live in the palace from then on. They were never hungry or cold again. In time the king and the young woman fell in love and were married.

Do you know, the journey went by as quick as a click of the fingers.

'Who told you that tale?' the mason asked his son.

'Mary. The woman from the bridge. I saw her in town.'

'Very good. What does she look like?'

Next day, the mason went to town. He found Mary and bought her a bite to eat.

'The only cure for a brainless man is for him to find himself a wife with brains enough for the both of them. I'm wondering if you would consider taking on my Jack.'

'I would.'

'That's settled then.'

In time, Mary married Jack, and they all lived together. Jack helped his father as best he could. He was strong and he was willing.

One day, a grand English lord visited the mason and his gormless son.

'I want a house built, a house that is worthy of me. No, not a house. I want a mansion. No, not a mansion, a palace! Can you do this?'

'I can.'

'There will be no finer a residence in the whole of England.'

The mason bowed.

Mary, standing by, frowned. Before Jack and his father set off, she said to her husband, 'Will you do something for me, Jack? Be kind to the rich man's servants. Treat them with respect, and they will return your kindness.'

'I will.'

Jack and his father travelled over the border and set to work. Such a place they made!

Turrets and towers and pediments and parapets and architraves and columns.

Every day, the lord would come and inspect the work. He'd nod and smile.

One day, he said, 'Very good, very good. But one more thing. I want a treasure room inside the palace, a secret room where I will keep my wealth. There must be no windows and only one way in or out. The door must have a spring and no handle on the inside.'

He who pays the piper calls the tune. After all, in his time the mason had been asked to do stranger things. When the palace was nearly finished, the lord's steward took them to one side.

'You are good men. You have shown us only respect, so I will share a secret. You know that new room? What do you suppose it is for?'

'He said to keep his wealth.'

'But do you remember what else he said? He said he would allow no finer residence in the whole of England. That is because you won't build another. That chamber will be your tomb. He will trick you into it, then lock the door and throw away the key.'

'Mary knew. She knew …'

That afternoon the mason went to the lord. 'My lord, I am worried that the land beneath your new home is boggy. I need an instrument called a long weight, to check that the walls are not subsiding. I will go home and fetch it. I will be back in a few days.'

'No!' interrupted the lord. 'I will send a servant.'

'My lord, with respect, that tool was given me by my master when I was an apprentice. It has been handed down from mason to mason since the time of King Solomon himself. I will not trust just anyone with it. That would be against the oath I swore to my guild. I will send my son.'

'No. Your son stays here. I will send mine.'

'Very well.'

The lord's son travelled to the mason's home. There was Mary.

'I have been sent for a long weight,' said the lord's son.

'Then come with me.' She led him inside. She lifted the lid of a chest. 'In there.'

He leant over the chest … she pushed him in, BAM! She slammed down the lid and turned the key. 'You heard long weight. I heard long wait!'

She wrote a letter to the lord. Unless he freed Jack and the mason and paid them their due, he'd never see his son again.

What could the lord do? He loved his son as much as the mason loved Jack. So he paid. They went home. Mary released the lord's son.

'Well done, Mary!' said the mason. 'I know Jack is in safe hands.'

He built a wonderful home for Jack and Mary – not as fancy as the lord's high hall, but cosy and comfortable. Eventually Jack and Mary had a daughter of their own. And they were in luck: she had Jack's looks and Mary's brains, not the other way around!

Tanwyn

In the days when wisdom was taught through proverbs and stories, there lived a father and son. Though they were poor, the father tried the best he could every day to teach his son the right way to live. Eventually the father grew sick. On his deathbed, he gave his son all the money he had – two sovereigns – and said:

'I have nothing more to teach you. The time has come for you to make your own way. The world is a strange place. There's a reason why God gave you two ears and one mouth. Watch and listen before you speak.'

He clutched his son's wrist, and whispered, 'Careful when you dig. A hole doesn't care whom it swallows.'

The young man's name was Tanwyn. Once he had buried his father, he had no choice but to seek his fortune.

He walked over stones, stiles and long miles. One morning he saw a beggar, his clothes tattered, his hat battered, shuffling toward him, his hand outstretched. 'Give me a sovereign and I will tell you something worth hearing!'

Tanwyn looked at the beggar and thought of his father's advice.

'Two sovereigns, one sovereign, there isn't much difference,' he thought. He reached into his pocket and gave the beggar a sovereign.

'Why take the new road when the bridge isn't broken on the old one?'

Tanwyn thanked the beggar and walked on. At the same time the next day, didn't he see another beggar, his clothes in rags, trembling from head to toe?

'Give me a sovereign and I will tell you something worth hearing!'

'One sovereign, no sovereigns. There isn't much difference,' replied Tanwyn, as he handed his last sovereign to the old man.

'If the birds are more beautiful, ignore the bells.'

Tanwyn thanked the old man and walked on. He

came to a beach. He took a stick and wrote in the sand his father's last words:

CAREFUL WHEN YOU DIG.

A HOLE DOESN'T CARE WHOM IT SWALLOWS.

Then he walked on.

That day, the king happened to be riding on the beach. He read the words in the sand and saw the young man walking away. The king called to him. 'Did you write this?'

'I did, your majesty.'

'You might be the answer to my problem. I want to hire a steward, someone to manage my estate and look after my money. I've tried to find a man I can trust, and I don't mind telling you, I didn't like the look of any of the men who offered to work for me. I wouldn't trust them with a loaf of bread, let alone my affairs. But you … reading this makes me wonder if you might be the man for the job. You know that to hurt another is to hurt yourself, and a wrongdoing comes back to destroy the wrongdoer. If I were to put you in charge of my land, my properties, my herds of sheep and pigs and cattle, what would you ask in the way of wages?'

'What I was worth, after you have seen my work.'

'A wise answer.'

And so that very day Tanwyn and the king travelled to his palace. They arrived late, and everyone was asleep. But the next morning there was uproar. Someone had stolen a brooch from the queen! Although all the doors and windows were locked at night, one window was found swinging open.

The head cook said, 'Your highness, beg your pardon for saying so, but it seems strange that the day after the new steward arrives the queen's brooch goes missing ...'

Tanwyn asked, 'Was the brooch kept hidden?'

'Of course!' said the king.

'I arrived at midnight. How would I have known where she kept it? I will find your thief, but to do it I will need ...' He whispered in the king's ear.

Tanwyn asked for a cockerel, a cooking pot and a candle. He took them into an empty room. He lit the candle and held it under the bottom of the pot. Then he told the servants to fetch the bird. He put the pot over the bird. He covered the windows and the door. When the room was as black as night, he said, 'Your highness, send your servants into the room one at a time. Each of them must put their hand on the pot. When the thief does so, the cockerel will crow.'

The servants were lined up outside. They entered the room one by one. The cockerel was silent. It so happened that the cook was the last to enter. In he went ... and out he came, smiling, for the bird had not made a sound.

'Your highness, if I may be so bold, there is another servant who should be tested.' He nodded at Tanwyn. 'That one.'

And so Tanwyn entered the dark room. Still no sound. He emerged after a few moments.

'Well?' said the king.

Tanwyn said to the servants, 'Show me your hands.' They turned up their palms. Every hand was black with the soot the candle had left on the pot ... except for the hands of the cook.

'He is the thief. He did not dare to touch the pot for fear that the cockerel would crow.'

The cook confessed. The brooch was found, the cook dismissed.

At first, the other servants were wary of this new steward who had seen off their friend, but Tanwyn soon earned their affection. He never passed judgement on their actions until he had heard their side of the story, whether the dispute be between the butler and the ploughboy. So when the first year was over, the king gave him a generous wage.

One time, the king called Tanwyn into his study. 'Perhaps you can help me. A nobleman has died suddenly, leaving land and property but no will. He had two sons. They are arguing over how to divide their inheritance between them. They have come to me for advice. I cannot resolve this fairly – they will know best which field is fertile, and which barren. Can you resolve this matter?'

Tanwyn went to the nobleman's mansion with the king. The two sons were summoned. Tanwyn pointed at the young man on the left. 'You divide the estate in two,' as the other son stepped forward to object, Tanwyn said to him, '… but you have first choice.'

Of course, the first son was careful to ensure that the estate was fairly divided.

The sons came to the palace a few months later. They asked to see not the king, but Tanwyn.

'We thank you for resolving our dispute so skilfully. We are like so many brothers – rivals as well as friends. This matter could have caused a rift between us for the rest of our lives.'

One time, the king's brother arrived in court, most distressed. When the king asked him what the matter was, he asked to speak to the king alone.

'Tanwyn will be present. He is my most trusted advisor.'

When the room was clear save for the three of them, the king's brother told his story.

'His highness instructed me to bring him twenty precious jewels, but on my way here I was delayed by a storm. Night came upon me. I needed to find somewhere to sleep. I was afraid that the treasure would be stolen from me whilst I slept, so I buried it in a field, then took a room at a local inn. Next morning, the jewels were gone.'

Tanwyn said, 'If your highness will allow me?'

The king bowed his head.

'This is what you must do ...'

The brother went to the farmer who owned the field where he had buried the jewels and said, 'May I share a secret with you? I am a merchant. I had a hundred jewels. I was being pursued, so a few nights ago I buried twenty of them in one of your fields. Now I must conceal the rest. Is it safe to hide them in the same place? Or should I bury them somewhere else?'

The farmer replied, 'Don't worry. It is quite safe to leave all of them in the field.' But he thought, 'When he discovers his twenty jewels missing, he won't put more there. If I were to restore the ones I have taken, he will leave even more for me to steal!'

That night, the farmer replaced the jewels he had stolen. Once he had gone, the brother retrieved his treasure.

The brother returned to the palace and said, 'Thank you, Tanwyn. You are as shrewd a man as ever I met.'

The king saw such respect in his brother's eyes. He felt a strange sensation …

Stories of Tanwyn's shrewd judgements spread far and wide. Time and again the king's subjects came to the palace to kneel before Tanwyn and thank him. One day the king thought, 'My people, my brother, my queen, they all revere Tanwyn. It is as if he is the king! They love him more than they love me.'

What was this feeling? Ah! It was envy. The respect shown to Tanwyn came from his actions, not from an inherited title. A secret mistrust began to kindle in the king's mind over weeks and months, until it was a flaming jealousy. The king convinced himself Tanwyn wanted the throne.

The king sent for a messenger, saying, 'Take this note to the blacksmith.'

The messenger did as he was bid.

The blacksmith read:

'The next man from the palace who comes to your forge is a traitor. Never mind that he is loved. No matter who he looks like, no matter what he says, he is a threat to the nation and you must throw him in the fire. I will repay your loyalty with a sack of gold.'

The king sent for Tanwyn. 'Deliver this sack of gold to the blacksmith. Go at once. Take the new road: you must be there by midday.'

When he came to the junction between the new road and the old one, Tanwyn saw the old bridge was intact. He remembered the first beggar's words. The old road was less direct. It took him through a forest. The clock chimed twelve times. He was about to rush when he heard birdsong so beautiful he was reminded of the second beggar's counsel. He stopped to listen.

Back at the palace the king waited until midday. 'Tanwyn must be dead by now,' he thought, but he had to make sure. He rode on his fastest horse by the new road to the blacksmith's forge. The moment he stepped through the door the blacksmith seized him and threw him in the fire.

CAREFUL WHEN YOU DIG.

A HOLE DOESN'T CARE WHOM IT SWALLOWS.

There is much truth in that saying.

As for Tanwyn, he lived wisely and well, helping whoever asked for his counsel.

37

The Blacksmith and the Devil

There was once a blacksmith. He was not a good man. When he wasn't drinking he was cursing. When he wasn't cursing he was arguing. When he wasn't arguing he was fighting.

His forge was a little Hell – hot, dark and full of cursing. Everyone was scared of him, but everyone needed him to mend their tools and shoe their horses. There was no telling what he would do from one moment to the next. Sometimes when he drank he flew into a rage and threw rocks at passers-by. Sometimes when he drank he was absurdly generous. One night he was leaning in the doorway of his forge watching a storm. An old man passed by, bent over, tottering on two sticks.

'Hey you!' cried the blacksmith. 'Come in from the rain!'

He wouldn't take no for an answer. He took the traveller by the shoulders and led him to the fire. He gave him food, a mug of tea …

The stranger ate and drank. He said nothing, and listened to the blacksmith's talk.

The blacksmith lavished gifts on the stranger. Food, good wine, a new pair of boots …

After a while the blacksmith went into the night to pee. When he turned back toward his forge, a fierce white light was blazing out of the doorway. The stranger had changed. He'd uncurled and doubled in size.

The blacksmith frowned at him. 'Who the devil are you?'

'Don't you recognise me?'

The blacksmith shook his head.

The stranger sighed. 'A clue – the big key on my belt?'

The blacksmith shrugged.

'I'm not surprised. You haven't been to church since your parents passed away. I'm Saint Peter, keeper of the key to the gates of Heaven! Once a year I walk the world to see if I can find any decent people on it. The first man who shows me kindness gets three wishes. This time it is you!'

'Three wishes?'

'Choose carefully. Think before you …'

'You see that chair over there?' bellowed the blacksmith. 'It's my chair. It belongs to me. But do I ever get to enjoy it? Never. Everyone who comes in flops down on it. From now on, if anyone sits in that chair, they don't get up until I say!'

'What? That's your wish? Don't you want to do something about all your terrible sins?'

'You see that hammer? The young lads steal it, swing it around their heads, and chuck it at one another for a dare. I've found it in ditches, farmyards, dung heaps … I wish if anyone except me tries to pick it up, it'll whack them in the face until I say stop.'

'Your second wish from me, Saint Peter, Apostle of Christ, author of The Acts of Peter, The Gospel of Peter, The Preaching of Peter, The Apocalypse of Peter, and The Judgment of Peter, is for a face-smashing hammer?'

'You see that sack? Those young lads are too quick for me. When I say, "Into my sack!", whoever I call will be trapped inside!'

Saint Peter shook his head. 'These are sorry, sorry excuses for wishes. I had hoped you might use one wish to undo some of your dreadful wrongs, but no. You'd rather wish for sticky furniture.' And he was gone.

Time passed. The blacksmith lived out his days drinking and cursing and fighting. His hair went grey, then white, then it fell out. His hands began to shake. Did age bring wisdom? It did not. So evil was he that one night while he pounded at his anvil there was a flash of light and a puff of smoke. Out of the fug came a gentleman in black. And when that gentleman lifted his top hat the blacksmith saw a pair of horns.

'What do you want?'

'You. You're showing me up. All your misdemeanours are making me look lazy. You're coming with me. Hell will be a home from home for you.'

'I'll go when I have finished this,' and he turned back to the forge to resume his work. The devil waited, and waited ...

Now the blacksmith was looking for something.

'What is it?'

'Can you see my hammer?'

'There!' The devil picked it up to hand it to the blacksmith and BAM! It split the devil's nose.

BAM! BAM! BAM!

It shattered his teeth.

'Make it stop!'

BAM!

One eye.

BAM!

The other.

BAM!

His jaw.

BAM BAM BAM!

'I beg you, please! I'll give you anything!' The devil reeled and staggered under the onslaught.

'One lifetime isn't enough. I want more. Give me another and I'll make it stop.'

'Yes!' cried the devil.

'You swear?'

'I swear! Now, please!'

'Stop!'

The hammer dropped from the devil's hand. There was a flash of light, a puff of smoke and the devil was gone.

Time passed. The seasons came and went and came and went. In the village, the old people died and the young people grew up. The blacksmith didn't change.

Then one day, a flash of light and a puff of smoke. 'Time's up! Come on!'

'I'll get my things. There, take the weight off your hooves.'

The devil sat. The blacksmith went back to the anvil.

'Hurry up! You said you would get your things,' cried the devil.

The blacksmith kept on hammering.

The devil shouted, 'Enough!' He tried to stand – and couldn't. 'What have you done? I'm stuck!'

'Thirsty work, this. I'm off down the pub. See you later. Or maybe tomorrow.'

After a few hours the devil, still stuck to the chair, bent double, burst into the pub. 'GET ME OUT OF THIS CHAIR!'

'Temper, temper ...' The blacksmith yawned. He put down his glass. He scratched his belly. 'Goodnight!'

He went to his bed. All night the devil screamed and cursed. The blacksmith slept through it all.

Next morning the devil gave in. 'You win! What do you want?'

'Another lifetime.'

'Agreed!'

'You swear?'

'I swear!'

'Then be off with you!'

The devil started to stand. There was a ripping sound. He stopped. A look of agony passed across his face ... He took a breath, then tore himself free, leaving the chair upholstered with red skin.

There! Gone.

Time passed. By now the blacksmith was shoeing

the horses of the grandchildren of the men he'd grown up with.

Then the devil appeared. This time he danced from foot to foot and looked about warily. 'Don't bother trying to trick me! I won't pick up – I won't even touch – anything! Just. Come. With. Me!'

'Into the sack!' The devil leapt head first.

'Now what?'

The blacksmith picked up his hammer.

BAM! BAM! BAM!

He drew up his boot.

STOMP! STOMP! STOMP!

BAM!

STOMP!

He called to the lads outside. 'Hey, you! Come in here. You take that stick, and you take that poker, and you hold on to this …'

They beat the sack all afternoon.

When the yells had stopped and there was only whimpering, the blacksmith asked the devil, 'Have you had enough?'

'I never want to see you again!'

'Then be gone!' shouted the blacksmith.

Time passed. Though the blacksmith's body didn't age, he grew tired. He lost interest in living. Everyone

he'd known had died long ago. He thought, 'I'd best go and see my old friend, Peter.'

So he found the ladder to heaven, and climbed.

He reached the pearly gates. Saint Peter was inside. 'What are you doing here?'

'I'm bored of the earth. I've done everything I want to do down there. I want to come in.'

'After all the dreadful things you've done?'

'I was kind to you!' the blacksmith barked.

'Look at my book! This page and the page opposite are about your life. On the left side I have written all your acts of kindness. On the right side I have written all your acts of selfishness. The good side – two entries. The selfish side spills over onto one, two, three more pages!'

'I repent.'

'Too late!' And Saint Peter turned away.

'Oh well, if heaven won't take me, I'd better go to the other place.'

Down to the earth the blacksmith went, and further down still. As he approached the gates of Hell, he called, 'Hey, it's me, the blacksmith! Let me in!'

He heard, 'Oh no! Lock the gates! Bar the windows!'

Bolts were slid across, shutters slammed shut. Up above, the devil leant over the wall. 'Don't you remember? I said I never want to see you again!'

'Heaven won't have me and neither will you! What am I supposed to do?'

'Not my problem!'

And so the blacksmith walks the world even now. Maybe you'll meet him some day.

The Cinder Girl
and her Cruel Sister

There once lived a poor farmer. Two daughters he had. It was hard for him to earn enough to feed them. He worked so much he didn't notice a dreadful crime under his own roof. His wife had died while giving birth to the youngest daughter. The eldest child secretly blamed her sister for their mother's death. On the sixteenth anniversary of that day, once their father had gone to the fields, the eldest daughter beat her sister and threw her in the coal hole.

'From now on, you will be silent! I'll kill you if you speak a word!'

That night the father found his youngest daughter weeping and filthy. 'What has happened?' he asked.

'She has lost her mind!' said the eldest daughter. 'She won't talk. She rolls in the ashes. It is all I can do to stop her mischief. What about my chores?'

The farmer was a decent man, but he knew nothing about children. This strange, silent child was one trouble too many. Every night he came home exhausted from his toil. He didn't have the time or the energy to see to her. What was he supposed to do? Perhaps she had lost her mind. Perhaps she was bewitched. How was he supposed to know? When he asked her why she was behaving so strangely, she said nothing. So embarrassed and ashamed was he that he hid the cinder girl away. He wouldn't let her go out. If anyone came to the house, he locked her in a cupboard.

It was a lonely life she led. Her only friend was a bird she fed in the yard.

One Sunday, the father and the eldest daughter came home from chapel.

'Guess who we saw at the service?' asked the father. 'Only the prince himself!'

'He looked at me,' said the eldest daughter, 'twice!'

'Perhaps you'd like to come with us next week?' asked the father.

The girl nodded her head eagerly, but the eldest cried, 'What? And have his highness learn I have a witless sister? Don't be ridiculous!'

The following Sunday came. The father locked the silent one in a cupboard and set off with his eldest daughter to chapel. The cinder girl wept so bitterly that two streams came from her eyes.

Then she heard a scraping sound. She looked up and saw the bird tapping at the window. She opened it. The bird dropped two keys into her hand.

One of the keys was for the cupboard. She was free! The bird flew back and forth between her and the front door, chirruping. The girl followed. Across the yard there was a tree that had grown out of her mother's grave. The bird led her to it. She found a keyhole in the trunk. She put the second key in the keyhole … click! A door opened into the tree. She found herself in a high-roofed chamber. Here was a bath of warm water, beautiful clothes, glittering shoes and a white horse. The girl took off her rags and washed herself from head to foot. She put on a shimmering dress and a pair of sandals, climbed onto the horse and set off.

Meanwhile, in the chapel, the congregation heard the sound of a galloping horse. They glanced back to the door and saw a beautiful stranger. One look was all it took: the prince fell head over heels in love with her.

The hubbub made the elder sister curious. The girl saw her cruel sister turning her head … she fled.

The following Sunday the same things happened. The father locked her in the cupboard. The bird came with the keys. The cinder girl washed herself and dressed in fine clothes. She went to church but fled for fear that her sister would recognise her. The prince grew sick with longing.

The Sunday after that, she wanted to meet the prince so much she stayed a moment too long and her sister recognised her. She glared. The cinder girl fled. In her haste to escape her sandal slipped from her foot.

The prince went from house to house, searching for his love. He tried the sandal on every young woman he met. One morning, while the father was out, the sisters heard the sound of the prince's horse approaching. The eldest daughter noticed that the cinder girl's foot was smaller. The eldest daughter wanted to be a princess so much that she bundled her sister into the coal hole, rushed to the kitchen, took a knife, hacked off her toes, wrapped her foot in bandage and slipped on a sock.

Knock! Knock!

The eldest sister went to the door. She greeted the

prince. She led him to the kitchen, trying not to limp. She tried on the sandal.

'It fits!' he said. 'But what's that red stain on your sock?'

'Nothing …'

'It's growing!' said the prince.

'Don't worry!'

'The whole sock is red and wet! Take it off, so we can dress the wound! Where's your family?'

'They are out!'

'Hello! Is anyone here? What is that noise?'

He opened the coal hole and saw, grimy and beautiful, the cinder girl.

'There you are!' said the sister. 'Whatever were you doing, hiding in the dark? Your highness, there's something wrong with my sister …'

'You think so? I think she is quite perfect.'

The wedding was arranged. When she was alone with her younger sister, the eldest whispered, 'Speak and I'll say you are a witch. I'll tell such lies about you that they'll call off the marriage.'

So the cinder girl was silent.

The cinder girl's wedding was blighted. Whenever the cinder girl was happy, she'd glimpse her sister and panic.

A year went by. The cinder girl fell pregnant. The elder sister said to their father, 'It is a pity our dear mother is not here to help her, but I will do the best I can!'

'Of course!' said the father.

Just as the cinder girl began her labour, into her bedchamber came her sister. 'Please leave us. I will see to everything. She wants her sister to help her, not strangers, isn't that right?'

The cinder girl, petrified, nodded her head. The sister shooed away the nurses and the servants.

The cinder girl gave birth to a lovely daughter. The sister said, 'It should have been you who died during labour, not our mother.'

She smuggled the baby out of the palace, abandoned it in the forest then replaced it with another bundle. She sent for the prince.

'Look!' She drew back the blankets to reveal the cinder girl cradling a newborn dog. 'I told you there was something wrong with her! She is a witch!'

He said to his wife, 'Tell me what happened?'

The cinder girl opened her mouth to explain, but she saw her sister behind him, and lost the courage to utter a word.

The prince was horrified, but he loved his wife so much that he told the world their child had died.

Another year went by. This time the cinder girl gave birth to a son. It all fell out the same way.

Again the sister abandoned the baby in the forest and replaced it with a newborn dog.

She said to the prince, 'You are so loyal to my sister! That is admirable, but think of the future of your kingdom. You need an heir to take the throne after your death. Even I, your wife's sister, can see you should find a new bride.'

'While my wife lives, there is not room in my heart for another.'

Again he told the world his child had been stillborn.

Another year. Another son. Again the sister pulled back the sheets to reveal the cinder girl holding a puppy.

'Please, save yourself! Speak to me!' exclaimed the prince.

But the cinder girl was too afraid.

The prince sighed and summoned a soldier. 'My wife is a witch,' he said. 'Take her into the forest and kill her. Tell no one.'

The soldier hid his horror and bowed. At dead of night he took the cinder girl into a clearing in the forest. He lifted his dagger … and stabbed his arm. He soaked a handkerchief with his blood.

'I will take this cloth to his highness. It will be proof that you are dead. But this means you can never return to the palace. If you do, we will both be put to the sword.'

The cinder girl bowed her head in thanks. Once he had gone she lay down in the grass and wept.

When the soldier returned to the palace with the bloody handkerchief, the cruel sister saw his wound and was suspicious. She slipped out to the forest to search for the body.

The cinder girl was awoken by her old friend the bird, chirruping in a tree above her. The bird flew down to her. The moment it touched her, the girl felt herself changing. Her ears grew, her limbs shrank, her dress, her shoes sloughed off. She was a sow now, a female pig. And not a moment too soon! Into the clearing came the cruel sister. She inspected the dress. She looked at the sow for a moment, then resumed her search.

For years the cinder girl lived in the forest in the shape of a beast, until one morning she chanced upon a little hut. Three children came bounding out, laughing with an old woodsman.

'Tell us again the story of how you found us!'

'It is like a fairy tale of old. Three times a bird woke me and led me through the night to a newborn baby! I searched for the one who had left you there, but all I found was a woman's footprints.'

'Was it our mother?'

'Why would she abandon us?'

'All I can say is, God moves in a mysterious way. The prince is sad in his palace, while I am glad in my shack!'

The cinder girl's heart leapt for joy! Her children were alive and safe, but she couldn't approach them because of the woodsman's dog. She had to watch from the safety of the woods.

Despite the cruel sister's efforts to win his heart, the prince still wept for his wife. By chance he heard the story of the foundlings in the forest, and found himself moved to tears. Those children were the same age as his own would have been had they lived. He resolved to seek out the foundlings and help them however he could.

But the cruel sister had also heard the story. She knew at once that the foundlings were her niece and nephews. She found the hut and waited. The children returned. She grabbed the woodsman's axe and ran at them. Just as she was about to strike, a sow leapt out of the undergrowth and bit her. The sister struck it a mortal blow.

The prince came galloping out of the woods. He saw the cruel sister and said, 'What are you doing here?'

'She tried to kill us,' said the little girl. 'The sow saved me.'

The prince turned to the children and his heart leapt. Had his misfortunes finally stolen his reason? The girl was the exact likeness of his wife! When the woodsman told the story of how a bird had led him to them in the woods, the prince knew the children were his own, and he knew who had made this misery.

The dying sow at their feet lifted its head and spoke, 'I want to lie with my mother.'

So they carried the sow's body to the tree and buried it there. As they walked away, the tree burst into flame. Out of the fire stepped the cinder girl, reborn. She embraced her husband and her children. The bird circled above them and sang for joy.

The Day it
Rained Potatoes

There was a woman once, and she had a foolish son, name of Tom. She said a newborn baby had more sense than him.

One time she said, 'I have to go out. Can you cook the dinner this afternoon? Fry the sausages and pour out the beer.'

So, that afternoon, Tom put the sausages in the pan and the pan on the fire. The sausages began to sizzle ...

'What else did I have to do? Oh yes, the beer!'

The barrel was in the cellar. Down he went. As he turned on the tap he heard the dog barking.

'Oh! I didn't tie him up! He'll be after the sausages!'

Sure enough, he reached the kitchen just in time

to see the dog bounding out of the front door with the string of bangers trailing out of his mouth.

'Come back!' He chased the dog three times around the yard. The dog leaped over a hedge. Tom, out of puff, went back to the farm.

'What's that smell?'

He looked down into the cellar … It was flooded with beer. He'd left the tap open.

'When my mum gets back she'll be hopping mad! Ah! I'll dry it up with this flour.'

He emptied three sacks of the best flour into the beer. When his mum came home, she found no dinner and a cellar full of glue.

'I have to take more care around him!' she thought.

She had saved up some golden coins, which she kept in a box. She thought, 'He can't be trusted. I'd better hide it.'

She showed it to Tom. 'You see these shiny things? They're just toys you used to play with when you were little. I'll bury them in the garden out of the way. Maybe one day they'll come in useful.'

One day, while she was out, Tom heard a knock at the door.

'Good morning!' said a pedlar. 'I've got some pots and pans I'd like to sell you.'

'I haven't got any money!'

'Have you got anything to swap for them?'

'Nothing. No wait! I've got some old toys …'

He dug them up. 'You want them?' he asked.

'Yes! I'll take them all off your hands.'

'Thank you!'

When his mum returned, she said, 'Where did those pots and pans come from?'

He answered proudly, 'I swapped them for those shiny toys you buried in the garden!'

'You did what! Who took them?'

'A pedlar.'

'I'm going after him!' And off she went.

'Hey! Don't leave me!'

She cried over her shoulder, 'If you're coming, make sure you pull the door to!'

She heard a scrape and a clatter. She looked back to see Tom dragging the door behind him. 'What have you done?'

'What you said! You said, pull the door, too!'

'I said, pull the door to … shut the door! You'll just have to bring it with us.'

They searched until night came. They found themselves in a dark forest. The path was so narrow, trees snagged their clothes.

'What's that noise?' asked his mother. 'Someone's coming! Quick, up the tree.'

'Shall I bring the door?'

'You'll have to! A door in the middle of the road will rouse suspicion.'

From up in the tree, they watched the pedlar and his friends gather below – and weren't they sharing out gold!

'Thieves!' she whispered. 'Not a sound!'

'But Mum, I have to … you know.'

'What? Why didn't you go before we left! You'll just have to wait.'

'I can't. I really need to – now.'

'Well, do it then.'

So he did.

Down below, the robbers exclaimed, 'That's odd. The sky is clear but it's raining.'

Then, Tom whispered, 'Mum …'

'Shh! What is it?'

'I want to … do the other thing now.'

'Wait!'

'I can't!'

'Do it then!' So he did.

The robbers said, 'The birds are big around here!'

'Mum …'

'What now!'

'I can't hold the door much longer.'

'Don't let go of it!'

'But it's heavy!'

He let go. Dummel-tummel-tummel-CRASH! The door fell on the forest floor. The robbers screamed and bolted, leaving their treasure behind.

As Tom's mum climbed down, she thought, 'What am I going to do with this gold so Tom doesn't give it away?'

Next morning, when Tom went out, his mum was on the roof, hiding behind the chimney. She pelted him with potatoes.

'Ow! Ow!' He ran back inside.

A few days later, he said, 'Where's all that gold?'

'What gold?'

'The gold you took from the robbers.'

'I didn't take any gold from the robbers,' shouted his mum.

'You so did!'

'So didn't!'

'That gold was mine,' complained Tom. 'I scared the thieves away, so it belongs to me!'

'There isn't any gold!'

'Right, that's it! I'm off to the judge!'

Tom ran to town. He said to the judge, 'My mum stole my gold!'

'Since when did you have gold?'

'Since the day it rained potatoes!'

The judge threw up his hands. 'Stop wasting my time with nonsense! Clear off!'

Tom and his mum lived off the robbers' treasure from that day.

The Secret of the Ring

Jack lived in a forest so vast that he had not ventured beyond the trees. He'd never seen anyone except his mother and father. His only friends were the birds and the animals. One day, he went to his parents and said, 'If I don't see a bit more of the world, I will go mad.'

His father said, 'Why? What's wrong with here? You don't know anything about the world outside. You think everyone and everything is nice and kind. Well, they're not!'

'How will I learn about the world if I stay here all my life?'

'Your pocket's moving!' said his father. 'What have you got in there?'

'A frog. I found it in the water bucket this morning, and saved it.'

'What did I say? The world will chew you up and spit you out!'

His mother said, 'Well then, Jack, if you've set your heart on walking the world, nothing I say will change your mind. Take this ring. If ever you are near death, take it off and blow on it.'

'I hope I never need to.'

'That is in God's hands.'

As he walked away, his father, on the roof of the cottage, shouted at him. 'You brainless chump! You'll be back with your tail between your legs.'

Jack walked and walked and walked until he heard a strange sound. He found a fledgling in the middle of the road. The fledgling was too weak to utter a squeak, but its mother in their nest up above was chattering frantically. Soft hearted Jack picked up the fledgling, put her back in the nest and walked on.

Night fell. He saw a light. When he came closer he saw it was from a fine house.

Front door or back? He didn't know. He had been told beggars went to the back door. Was he a beggar? He had no money and nowhere to sleep, so he supposed he was.

The servant who opened the door took pity on him. He gave Jack a chair by the fire, a bowl of soup, a hunk of bread and a bucket of water for the frog. As he sat in the kitchen, the daughter of the house walked in. She was the first young woman Jack had seen. He fell head over heels in love with her.

Whatever it was she had come into the kitchen for was forgotten in a moment. She couldn't take her eyes off Jack.

Then her father joined them. He saw at once his daughter gaping open-mouthed at a beggar, and the beggar gawping back.

'Please sir, can I have a job? I can do anything!'

'Anything? Is that so? If tomorrow morning there's a lake outside the house, and if on the lake there's a fleet of galleons, and if the leader of the fleet fires a cannon as the clock chimes eight, and if the cannonball from that cannon breaks the leg of my daughter's bed, then I'll think about letting you stay. But if you don't do this one little thing, then I'll have your head.'

Jack was shown to a bedroom. He said to his pet frog, 'Oh my friend, what should I do? If I run away I will leave behind the love of my life. If I stay here I will die.'

'Kro! Kro!' said the frog, then it leapt from the bucket into Jack's lap, burrowed into Jack's pocket and emerged with his mother's ring.

'Of course! I'll never be nearer death than now!'

Just before eight he blew on it. Out hopped three little red men. They bowed and said, 'What is your command, master?'

'I want a lake outside this house. On the lake I want a fleet of galleons, I want the leader of the fleet to fire a cannon as the clock chimes eight, and the cannonball from that cannon to break the leg of the bed of the daughter of this house.'

'It shall be done. Go to sleep.'

Jack did. He slept through the clock chiming, the servants gasping, the gentleman running to the window, the boom of the cannon, the crash of the window and the crack of the bed leg.

The gentleman burst into Jack's bedroom. 'Young man, there's more to you than meets the eye! Come and have breakfast with me!'

From then on, Jack could do no wrong. Jack and the gentleman's daughter were wed. The gentleman gave Jack a mansion to live in, fine clothes to wear, a horse to ride on and a servant of his own.

But the servant hated his new master. Who was this tramp and what was his secret? How had this ignorant farm boy conjured such wonders? While Jack was asleep, he searched Jack's clothes. Nothing. No magic book or wand. But what about that ring?

One time, while Jack was in the bath, the servant saw the ring on the bedside table. He reached for it. It slipped from his fingers onto the dusty floor. He scooped it up and blew on it.

Out hopped three little red men.

'What is your command, master?'

'Master, is it?' exclaimed the servant. 'Fly this mansion to the other side of the world. Leave only Jack behind.'

One moment Jack was in the bathroom, the next he and his bath were in the middle of a field! His mansion had gone! His father-in-law came running.

'What has happened? Where is your house? Where is my daughter?'

'Someone must have stolen my magic ring!'

'Where did they go?'

'I wish I knew!'

'Find them!' cried his father-in-law. 'You have a year. If you fail, your head will be forfeit!'

So poor Jack had to tramp the length and breadth of Wales searching for his wife.

One morning, he reached into his sack and found a crust and a handful of crumbs. He heard a shrill squeal. He searched for the source of the sound and saw a remarkable sight. A cat had cornered three mice. The first mouse had a wooden leg. The second had a bandage over her ears. The third had a bandage over her eyes. They fought bravely but it was hopeless. Their tails were trapped under her paw.

Soft-hearted Jack ran at the cat. She hissed and spat and bounded off.

'Thank you,' said the mouse with the wooden leg. 'We owe you our lives. We will serve you faithfully from this moment.'

Jack wondered what possible use a blind mouse, a deaf mouse and a mouse with a wooden leg could be to him, but he didn't want to offend them, so he told them his story.

'We will find the thief. We will steal back the ring. Then you can wish your wife and your house and everything back.'

'Kro! Kro!'

'Who said that?' said the mice.

'My pet frog,' said Jack. 'He wants to go with you, but you don't know where to look.'

Jack heard another voice. 'I know.'

He looked about. 'Where are you?'

'Here.'

On a branch above their heads sat a starling. 'I, too, owe you my life. Do you remember, as you set off, you saved a fledgling? I was that fledgling. It was your servant who stole your ring. On my travels I saw

your house. Your home is so far from here, by the time you reached it the year would be over. And your servant has used the magic of the ring to set many traps for you.

'An army protects your home day and night. When they see you coming they will kill you.

'You can only enter through one door, and that door is locked. If you unlocked it, it would slam shut on you the moment you tried to pass through.

'As soon as anyone crosses the threshold a terrible screaming fills the house. No one can bear to hear it. Even if you could, it would still be impossible to find the ring because when the screaming begins your servant's bedroom is plunged into a thick darkness.

And your servant sleeps with the ring in his mouth.'

'It is hopeless,' cried Jack.

The mice conferred in a huddle, then the mouse with the wooden leg bowed to the starling.

'If you would be kind enough to take us to that place, and if you, Jack, were to give us a twist of pepper then we will do the rest.'

'Kro! Kro!' said the frog.

What had Jack to lose?

The three mice and the frog jumped onto the starling's back. She lifted them and carried them far across the sky. She set the mice outside Jack's house. When she had done so she fluttered up into the face of the sentry above. While he was distracted, the first mouse picked the door lock with his wooden leg. They pulled the door open, but as soon as they had done so it began to swing closed again. The first mouse wedged his wooden leg into the gap, giving the other two enough space to wriggle through.

An awful screaming pierced the air. The soldiers searched for the thieves who had crossed the threshold, but they didn't notice two tiny mice. The blind mouse curled up in a ball, overcome by the dreadful sound, but the deaf mouse rolled him to the servant's bedchamber.

Once inside the chamber all was silent and full of a thick blackness. The dark was no obstacle to the blind mouse: she lived in it. She listened for the servant's breathing, climbed onto his bed and scattered the pepper under his nose.

ACHOO! The ring flew from his mouth. The blind mouse heard where it landed and scooped it up. She ran to the deaf mouse who rolled her through the screaming. Once they had safely squeezed through the gap, the first mouse removed his wooden leg and the door slammed shut.

As they flew home the mouse with the wooden leg said, 'Thank goodness for me! Without me you would never have stolen the ring. I got you inside.'

'Yes, but without me,' said the second mouse, 'we would never have reached the bedroom.'

'I think you'll find that without me,' said the third mouse, 'the ring would still be in the servant's mouth!'

'Stop fighting!' said the first. 'I'm the hero of this adventure!'

'No, I am!'

'I am!'

The three of them tugged and pulled at the ring until it fell from their grasp into the sea below.

'We've lost the ring!'

'Kro! Kro!' said the frog, and he leapt into the ocean. The starling circled until at last the frog broke the surface with the ring in his mouth.

Jack, sitting under the tree, saw a speck in the sky. The speck became the starling. She had the mice and the frog on her back and the ring in her claw.

Jack blew on the ring. The three red men appeared.

'What is your command, master?'

'Bring home my house, my wife, all – save my servant.'

The servant awoke in the middle of an empty field. All his clever traps had failed.

Jack saw the front door of his house open and out came his wife with a baby in her arms. He sent for his old mother and father and they had a feast. There was good food for Jack and his family, seed for the starling, cheese for the mice and weed for the frog.

Jack's father said, 'I always knew he was destined for greatness.'

A Fib to Finish

Yesterday morning, at six o'clock in the evening, I was sailing through the sky in a little boat when I saw two men on horseback riding a pigeon. I said to them, 'Have you seen my sister?'

'What does she look like?'

'She has a long white beard.'

'No, we haven't seen her. Ask the man down there. You can't miss his house, it is all by itself in a row.'

So I went to the house and knocked on the door. He was a big man, so big he jumped out of a thimble. He shook me by the hand.

'Would you like some breakfast?'

'No thank you,' I said, so he gave me some. He gave me a plate piled high with lumps of steaming crunchy beer and a drink of mashed potato. Some crumbs from the beer fell under the table. I heard a noise, looked underneath, and there, nibbling the crumbs of the beer, was a giraffe.

I said, 'I am going to strangle that giraffe!'

The man said, 'No, that's a very useful giraffe. Only yesterday it went out in the garden, caught a rabbit and ate it. If you don't believe me, ask the rabbit.'

So I went outside into the garden. I saw a lovely apple tree covered in bananas. I saw a hippopotamus sitting on some donkey's eggs to hatch them out. I saw a man who was blind, a man who couldn't talk, a man with no legs, and a man with no clothes on. The blind man saw the rabbit. The man who couldn't talk said, 'Hey look, there's a rabbit!' The man with no legs chased the rabbit around the garden until he caught it and kicked it, then he gave it to the man with no clothes on who put it in his pocket.

I saw some deer. I thought, 'There's nothing I like eating more than a nice bowl of cornflakes.'

So I put an arrow into my bow and loosed the arrow through the air. The arrow missed the deer and hit a fish who was going past on a motorbike. With that fish I made the best apple pie you have ever tasted.

78

❦

Enough for one,
Too much for two,
Nothing for three.
What is it?

❦

It is a secret …